MW01154101

The TALLEST BRIDGE in the World

A Story for Children About Social Anxiety

by
Ellen Flanagan Burns

illustrated by
Anthony Lewis

Magination Press • Washington, DC • American Psychological Association

For Kaelyn—EFB

For Louise, with love—AL

Published by
MAGINATION PRESS®
An Educational Publishing Foundation Book
American Psychological Association
750 First Street, NE
Washington, DC 20002

Magination Press is a registered trademark of the American Psychological Association.

For more information about our books, including a complete catalog, please write to us, call 1-800-374-2721, or visit our website at www.apa.org/pubs/magination.

Book design by Gwen Grafft
Printed by Lake Book Manufacturing, Inc., Melrose Park, IL

Library of Congress Cataloging-in-Publication Data

Names: Burns, Ellen Flanagan, author. | Lewis, Anthony, 1966- illustrator.
Title: The tallest bridge in the world : a story for children about social anxiety /
  by Ellen Flanagan Burns ; illustrated by Anthony Lewis.
Description: Washington, DC : Magination Press, [2017] | "American
  Psychological Association." | "An Educational Publishing Foundation Book." |
  Summary: Thomas's parents take him to speak with a counselor, who provides
  him with tools for coping with feeling uncomfortable around other people.
Identifiers: LCCN 2017000259 | ISBN 9781433827600 (hardback) | ISBN
  1433827603 (hardback)
Subjects: | CYAC: Social phobia—Fiction. | Counseling—Fiction. | Middle
  schools—Fiction. | Schools—Fiction.
Classification: LCC PZ7.B9366 Tal 2017 | DDC [Fic]—dc23 LC record available
  at https://lccn.loc.gov/2017000259

Manufactured in the United States of America
10 9 8 7 6 5 4 3 2 1

Table of Contents

Dear Reader,

Many people feel self-conscious, just like Tommy. I know I've felt that way. I used to constantly wonder things like *"What will they think of me?"* or *"Will I look silly?"* These kinds of thoughts distract us, and can sometimes make us feel so nervous that we avoid situations that might be fun.

Tommy wonders why he gets so nervous in front of the class or ordering his food in a restaurant. He notices that other people don't panic like he does when he has to do something in front of people. Even Patrick, who is shy, volunteers in class sometimes! Why can't he?

It can be useful to learn about the kinds of thoughts that make us feel nervous and the kinds of thoughts that don't (thoughts lead to feelings, so we're happier when our thoughts make sense). Maybe you'll recognize some of the thoughts that plague Tommy...

People are looking at me closely. Nope, nobody is looking at us any closer or in more detail than anybody else. That would take too much energy!

Things are either good or bad. Nope, most of the time it just is what it is. Not everything has to be good or bad!

Mistakes are embarrassing. Nope, mistakes are totally normal. In fact, they don't mean much, other than, well...you're human. Everyone makes mistakes sometimes!

We should hide our flaws or quirks from others. Nope, nobody is looking at our flaws through a magnifying glass anyway, and besides, it just is what it is. Sometimes those quirks are the things we like most about our friends!

Rose gives Tommy tools to overcome his fear of doing things in front of people. Tommy even discovers one on his own! You can use the tools too. With a lot of courage, Tommy decides to test them out and discovers that his nervous fears are pretty flimsy. The more he practices, the easier it gets, and Tommy is finally on his way to having fun and living life without the magnifying glass.

With these new tools, and a whole lot of practice, you can too...

Your friend,

Ellen

Chapter One

Thomas

"Get ready for the morning warm-up," Miss Clark said to her math class as she posted a few problems for them to practice. Thomas Tuggle got right to work. He liked math and liked trying new problems. But he hated the old familiar feelings in his body; his face felt hot and was probably turning red, his hands felt sweaty, and his heart was racing. He knew what was coming. Sure enough, after a few minutes, Miss Clark asked for volunteers to go to the board and explain their answers.

Thomas didn't volunteer. He never did. He was uncomfortable being the center of attention. "I hope she doesn't call on me," he thought, even though he knew his answers were right. Thomas wished he had the power to be invisible. He would use it now.

He glanced around the room. Everyone else seemed fine. Even Patrick seemed okay, and Patrick was shy. Thomas wondered why *he* was so different. Why was going to the board so hard for *him*? He hoped nobody could see how nervous he felt. It was embarrassing.

Luckily for Thomas and Miss Clark, a lot of hands shot up, eager to show their work. Miss Clark picked Patrick first—quiet Patrick. "Oh no," Thomas thought. "When he gets up there, he'll feel like I do." Thomas expected to see Patrick get red in the face and stumble on his words. "He'll probably talk really fast so he can get it over with," he assumed. But none of those things happened. Patrick was the same as always.

Then Miss Clark picked Bill, Thomas's best friend. Thomas thought Bill seemed so comfortable in front of the class, like he was talking to a room full of friends. Even when he got part of the problem wrong, Bill just rolled with it, like it didn't bother him. Thomas wished he could be like that.

*   *   *

After school, Thomas and Bill walked home and met Mrs. Tuggle digging in her garden. A steady breeze swayed the trees, blending the colors of the autumn leaves.

"The leaves remind me of a watercolor painting," Mrs. Tuggle said. "Isn't it pretty? The boys looked around at the colorful picture and had to agree.

"Everything used to be green," Thomas said.

"That's true. How was school today?" Mrs. Tuggle asked.

"Awesome," Bill replied.

Thomas shrugged. "Okay, I guess." He caught a leaf that gently floated from above. He wanted to tell his mom about his feelings, but didn't know how.

"Swim team sign-ups are next month," she reminded them.

They had talked about joining the winter team, but now Thomas wasn't so sure. He didn't like how the swimmers waited on the side of the pool to start the races. Everyone would stare at him. And what if he lost the race? Or what if he looked silly when he swam? That would be embarrassing.

"I can't wait," Bill said. "Are you joining, Tommy?"

Thomas shrugged. "I don't know yet."

"It'll be fun," Bill said, then continued on his way home. Thomas sat with his mom for a few minutes and watched her plant a yellow mum. He thought about swim team and school. He remembered some of the group projects coming up and got a knot in the pit of his stomach.

"Mom, I hate going to school," he confided. "It's worse than last year. I think I'd rather play with a bunch of snakes." That was saying a lot because Thomas hated snakes.

Mrs. Tuggle put down her shovel and sat next to him. She hoped things would be better this year. Thomas did too. "What's going on?" she asked.

"I get so nervous when people expect me to do stuff."

Thomas felt nervous when he did a lot of things. Even things he liked to do. He liked playing games and having fun with his friends, but not at birthday parties. Birthday parties made him feel uncomfortable. Would they have to play games in front of everyone? Would he look silly? Sometimes he got so upset beforehand that he couldn't even go. And he liked hanging out with his classmates, but despised group projects—they were a lot of pressure. Would he do a good job? What would his group think of him? And eating out with his family was fun…until it was time to give his order. He didn't like how the waitress stared at him. His face always turned red. Did he look weird? Did his voice sound funny? So he usually looked down at the table, and luckily his mom usually ordered for him. And now swim team...it seemed exciting, but the thought of messing up and embarrassing himself was too upsetting.

Mrs. Tuggle said, "We all feel nervous sometimes. I used to feel nervous when I didn't know the answers in school."

"I feel nervous even when I know the answers," Thomas explained. "And when we have to work in groups, I can never think of what to say." Thinking of what to say wasn't difficult for Thomas when he wasn't nervous.

"What do you think will happen?" Mrs. Tuggle asked.

"I don't know," Thomas said. "I feel like I stand out like a sore thumb."

This had been going on for a while. "Sometimes it feels like we're on a stage performing, and we worry our audience won't like us. Most of us feel that way from time to time," Mrs. Tuggle explained. "Dad and I are going to help you with this. We're going to meet a therapist named Dr. Goode—everyone calls her Rose."

Thomas liked the idea of getting help, but he was nervous too. What would Rose think of him?

Chapter Two

Through a Magnifying Glass

Thomas and his parents met Rose in her cool office with lots of books, a desk, and comfy chairs. She collected lamps and so far she had six, in all different shapes and sizes. Thomas's favorite was made out of light blue-ish green glass that you could see through. It reminded him of sea glass from the beach.

Rose seemed nice as she listened to Thomas and his parents. She understood what Thomas was going through. She said this was something called Social Anxiety Disorder, and that it was pretty common. She even had other clients struggling with the same thing; kids like Thomas, and even some adults!

"It's when we feel like we're being judged by others," she explained. "And who can relax when they're feeling judged?"

That made sense to Thomas. "Not me. When I have to do things in front of people, it's embarrassing."

"What makes it embarrassing?" Rose asked gently.

"I think...I probably look weird somehow. Or I think I might say something wrong or do something wrong. And I always wonder if my face will turn red or if my voice sounds funny."

"Those are upsetting thoughts," Rose agreed. "So what do you do?"

"I get really nervous and then I clam up," Thomas admitted.

"That's understandable. You're not alone. In fact, many people feel like you do. The good news is this is something you *can* get over," she said.

Thomas felt relieved that Rose understood.

"I'll show you the way. We're going to build your toolbox and fill it with new skills to help you."

Thomas liked the idea of having tools to help him when he needed it most.

"So, think hard..." Rose prompted. "When you do things, how often do you actually do something embarrassing?"

Thomas shrugged. "I don't know, sometimes... probably not much," he guessed.

"So it could happen, but it's not likely."

"I guess not...but I don't take the chance very much."

"If you did embarrass yourself, like if you made a mistake or looked silly, what do you think would happen?" Rose asked.

"People wouldn't like me."

"Have you ever seen anyone else do something embarrassing?"

Thomas thought. Nothing came to mind right away. Finally, he remembered something. "Kevin tripped on his way up to the board to show his work and some people laughed."

"What did you think of him then?" Rose wondered.

"Well, nothing really. I figured his foot got caught on his chair. Oh yeah, and Tim stutters sometimes."

"Is Tim a friend?"

"Yeah, he's really nice."

"When he stutters, what do you think of him?"

Thomas shrugged. "That's just what Tim does sometimes."

"So, you like Kevin and Tim anyway?"

"Yeah, but it's different with me. People might not like the way I am."

"So you think people are looking at you closer," Rose said. She picked up a magnifying glass on her desk and looked at Thomas through the lens. Her eye looked ten times bigger.

Thomas laughed. He could see where this was going. Maybe he was being unfair...expecting the worst of people. He shrugged.

"Well, since they haven't given you a reason to believe that they look at you closer, then maybe they don't. Maybe most people are just like you...

and they don't look at you any closer than you look at them," Rose said.

Thomas thought about it. He knew it made sense, but for some reason he still had a hard time believing it.

Rose handed him the magnifying glass. "So when you think people are focusing in on your voice, or on something you said or did, maybe they really aren't."

Thomas's mom remembered a party she went to. "I joined a group of people doing yoga on the grass, but I wasn't dressed for yoga. Suddenly, in the middle of my Downward Facing Dog, I heard a loud *'rrrrip'* and discovered my pants split right up the back."

Thomas thought that was the worst thing in the world. He couldn't imagine anything more embarrassing. "Did you run away?"

"I thought about it for a second, but then I just laughed instead!" Mrs. Tuggle smiled again thinking about it.

Thomas couldn't imagine laughing about that. He would look like a fool. "What did the other people do?"

"Some of them giggled, but most of them continued doing yoga."

Thomas thought he would die if people laughed at him.

"It's okay, I had to admit it was funny," Mrs. Tuggle said. "A couple girls told me embarrassing things that happened to them. Like how one of them went to school wearing one black shoe and one brown shoe. I realized I wasn't the only one that embarrassing stuff happened to. Then my friend ran inside and found a pair of shorts for me to change into, and I had fun for the rest of the party." Mrs. Tuggle smiled. "Do you think any less of me now?"

"No." In fact, Thomas felt closer to his mom.

Rose said, "Mrs. Tuggle, you could have felt bad about the whole thing, but things like that happen sometimes and they don't really mean much, just like it didn't really mean much when Kevin tripped or Tim stuttered. You could have decided that people thought you were weird, but you couldn't read their minds so...who knows?"

"Right. I just assumed it was no big deal, because if it had happened to someone else, I wouldn't think much of it."

Thomas relaxed a little knowing that nobody was looking at him any closer than anyone else. He imagined placing a big magnifying glass into his toolbox. It was his first tool. He called it the *Magnifying Glass*.

Chapter Three

Dominoes

Rose went on. "You see our thoughts, feelings, and behaviors are like a game of Dominoes… the first domino is a *thought*, the second domino is a *feeling* and the third domino is a *behavior*. Each domino leads to the next. *Ping, Ping, Ping!*

"Here's an example…as I'm learning to play tennis, I hit the ball way out of the park—oops! Then I have the thought, 'It's okay to make mistakes,' *Ping!* which causes me to feel better, *Ping, Ping!* which causes me to practice more tennis. *Ping, Ping, Ping!*

"Social anxiety works in the same way, only the dominoes lead you in a different direction. Here's an example: as I'm learning a new dance in school, I have the thought, 'I look weird,' *Ping!* which causes me to feel anxious and get sweaty hands, *Ping, Ping!* which causes me to stop dancing. *Ping, Ping, Ping!*

"So, if I don't want to play the social anxiety game, what do I do?" Rose asked.

"Stop the first domino from falling!" Thomas said.

"Right! Change my thought!"

Thomas got it. "Our thoughts are really important, because they lead to everything else." He never realized how important they were before.

"Yes! It's like the detective whose ideas kept leading him down the wrong path," Rose said. "When a bird landed on a tree branch, he announced, 'A small airplane just landed on that man's arm!' And when a rainbow appeared in the sky, he announced, 'That's the tallest bridge in the world!' He noticed his thoughts weren't making sense, they weren't adding up. 'Airplanes don't land on people, and bridges aren't *that* tall,' he knew. So he got his eyes checked and sure enough he needed glasses."

"Then he could see clearly," Thomas said.

"Yes, he was relieved to see the pretty birds and beautiful rainbows again!"

Thomas smiled.

Rose said, "Be a good detective…notice your thoughts and see if they make sense."

"How?"

"When you feel anxious and your hands are sweaty, you can ask yourself, 'What am I thinking right now? Ah, yes, I'm thinking that…"

"…that other people aren't going to like the way my voice sounds or maybe they'll notice something weird about me."

"Then ask yourself…'Does this really make sense? Are people really looking at me that closely?'"

"Probably not."

"Then change that thought it into a more truthful one."

Thomas understood. "Like this? I have a thought that Joey and Bob are going to think my voice sounds funny when I talk in our math group. Hmmm. That's an interesting thought I'm having about Joey and Bob."

"Right! Now ask yourself if it really makes sense," Rose said.

"…let's see…it doesn't really make sense because Joey and Bob are smart and nice. They've never said anything about my voice before."

"So what's a more truthful thought?" Rose asked.

"Joey and Bob are probably thinking about other things…like solving the math problems, and they'll be glad if we can all work together. They're probably not thinking about my voice at all."

"You got it!" Rose said. "And how does that new thought make you feel?"

"Much better." Thomas said. He felt proud of himself and a little excited.

"Noticing your thoughts is another tool for your toolbox."

"I'll call it my *Domino* tool," Thomas said. He imagined a giant domino falling into another domino, with a *Ping*. "But what if I *still* can't be myself?"

"A good detective also tests out his ideas to see if they're correct."

"So…just be myself and see what happens?"

"Yes! And if you had to guess, what do you think would happen?"

"I'd probably see that nothing bad happens— just like airplanes don't really land on people and bridges aren't *that* tall."

"You would discover that you're okay just the way you are."

"Even if I feel shy and don't know what to say?"

"Yup! It's okay to have those moments, many of us do."

"Even if I blush?" This was something Thomas still worried about.

"Yes! Most people don't think blushing is a bad thing, in fact they don't think much of it at all."

Thomas thought it over. "I guess my fears are *not* very trustworthy. They make me feel like there's something wrong with me, when there isn't...like I'm under a magnifying glass, when I'm not."

"Excellent detective work!" Rose said.

Chapter Four

The Perfect Baker

"Would you like to hear the story about the perfect baker?" Rose asked at his next visit. Thomas nodded.

"He made the best desserts and was known all around the world for his pies, cakes, and cookies... but he also made muffins, brownies, and custards... and even fancy things like macaroons and petit fours. He won awards for his flaky pie crusts and his moist cakes, and his decorations won awards for being so beautiful. Everything he did turned to gold...or so it seemed. The truth was, not every cake turned out light and fluffy; sometimes they were hard like bricks, and he burned a whole batch of caramel at least twice a week. Caramel can burn quickly, he learned.

"He didn't want his customers to know that he made mistakes, so when he made a batch of gingerbread men with a little too much ginger in them, he threw them away. He did the same thing when he made cupcakes and added too many chocolate chips.

Luckily, he made his mistakes when nobody was there to see. But after a while the pressure got to him and he began to feel anxious.

"Then one day the worst thing in the world happened. In the middle of a busy day, with a long line of customers winding out the door and down the street, the baker left a batch of sugar cookies in the oven too long!"

"Well, that's not so bad," Thomas said.

"It was to the baker! As his customers were congratulating him on his latest award, he got a whiff of the overcooked cookies. He grabbed his oven mitts and dashed to the oven, but it was too late; some of the cookies were a little burned around the edges. 'They're not good enough,' he thought, so he raced them to the garbage.

"Just as he was about to throw them away, his customers yelled, 'Wait! Can we nibble them while we wait?'

"The baker was afraid to let them eat the cookies because they might think he 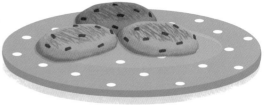 was a bad baker! He hesitated. 'They'll never come back again!' he told himself. The customers asked again, so the baker reluctantly placed the cookies on a pretty dish and set them out as samples. As he watched them nibble, his heart raced and his hands shook.

"'Hmm, not bad! Thanks!' they said.

"'But, they're not the best I can make!' the baker assured them.

"'They're not your best, but that's okay.'

"'*Huh?*' The baker couldn't believe his ears."

"He thought they'd be disappointed in him for making a mistake," Thomas said. "But they weren't."

"Right, because they knew he was more than his mistakes, and a few mistakes didn't mean he was a bad baker."

"Yeah, he was still a great baker and a nice person and everything else that he was."

"So from then on, the baker relaxed and started having fun again. And when he made a mistake here and there, he didn't worry about it. He knew his customers would always come back for more.

"This idea that everyone makes mistakes is another tool for your toolbox," Rose said.

"I'll call it my *Nobody's Perfect* tool," Thomas replied. Thinking of the incredible baker's hat would help him remember.

Chapter Five

It Is What It Is

"In fact, sometimes our little imperfections are the good stuff...they can be really wonderful," Rose said. "Like the girl named Ellie, who was born with ears that stuck out kind of far. 'You have your father's ears,' everyone told her since the day she was born. Ellie thought she had the best dad in the world, and she liked having ears like his. In fact, they made her feel pretty.

"'You'll have excellent hearing, just like me!' her dad joked. Ellie laughed.

"Then one day some of the kids called her names, like 'Elephant Ears' and 'Dumbo.' Ellie felt embarrassed. She decided her ears must be ugly for some reason, so she stopped liking them."

"Aw, that's too bad," Thomas said.

Rose agreed. "So she grew her hair long and wore little hats sometimes. That seemed to do the trick for a while, but Ellie wasn't happy—she was always worried her ears would show, and deep down,

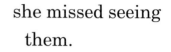

she missed seeing them.

"Then she discovered she could actually wiggle her ears, just like her dad could. 'Wow, this is cool!' Ellie thought. When she showed her best friend, her friend said, 'I wish I could do that!' That made Ellie's day. But when she showed the other kids, some of them laughed. That upset her."

"Her feelings go up and down…" Thomas said.

"…with everyone's opinion." Rose nodded.

"Finally Ellie didn't know what to think anymore. So she told her mom what some of the kids said, and to her surprise her mom just shrugged like it didn't mean much. She said, 'I bet if you asked a bunch of people if they liked spaghetti and meatballs, you would get a lot of different answers too. It depends on the person.'"

"Good point!" Thomas said.

"Right then Ellie realized that what other people thought of her ears was *their* business, not hers. And since *she* liked her ears, she stopped worrying about it. She started wearing pretty earrings with her hair up and rarely thought about it again."

"I like that ending," Thomas said.

"Ellie's ears are like my laugh," said Mrs. Tuggle.

"Yeah, my mom's laugh is loud." Thomas smiled at his mom apologetically. "And sometimes it's embarrassing," he admitted.

"I understand," Rose said. "I used to be embarrassed when my mom wore her bright pink sandals. But just because we have a thought about something, doesn't make it right or wrong…sometimes a thought is just a thought."

"So my laugh isn't necessarily good *or* bad," Mrs. Tuggle said.

"Exactly—it just *is what it is*," Rose said. "Can you think of any other examples of how *it is what it is*?"

"My friend Kaelyn has curly hair, like ringlets," said Thomas. "She says it's hard to control."

"Sounds awesome. I bet her curls have a mind of their own," Rose said. "What else?"

"My friend Bill likes to volunteer for clubs and sports, and he gets really busy!"

"That's what happens sometimes," said Rose.

"Patrick is shy and quiet, but he's funny too."

"Some people are quieter than others and some people are more talkative," Rose added.

"*It is what it is,*" Thomas agreed. Thomas liked Patrick.

"Chris gets around in a wheelchair, but nothing ever bothers him."

"He sounds like a patient person."

"He is. And his wheelchair *is what it is.*"

Then, Thomas had a thought. "I still think my voice sounds weird sometimes." Thomas knew it didn't make sense, but the thought persisted.

"That's the first domino," Rose reminded him.

"And it makes me feel nervous," Thomas replied. "And then I don't want to talk."

"So, tell yourself a new thought, one that's more truthful."

"My voice *is what it is,*" Thomas said. "Besides, nobody's looking at it through a magnifying glass."

"Well done! And how do you feel now?"

"Much better." Thomas liked this new way of thinking, because it made more sense. But he could see it was going to take some practice.

He went on, "Sarah's good with technology."

"That's her thing," Rose said.

"She even helps the teachers sometimes. Ed's hilarious but sometimes the teachers have to remind him to get back on track."

"You share the same sense of humor with Ed," Rose said.

"Yeah, he makes me happy. And Tim stutters, but it's no big deal. I think he gets speech therapy."

It was fun thinking of examples of how *it is what it is*. Thomas liked that not everything had to be *good or bad*. He thought of Ellie and her ears. "I'm going to call this my *It Is What It Is* tool."

Thomas kept going. "Chad uses a computer to write because he doesn't have very good handwriting. And Brian sings...all the time!"

"*It is what it is*!" Thomas and Rose repeated together.

Thomas began to laugh and the next thing he knew, he was blushing. He looked away. "See? When I blush, it's the worst thing ever."

Rose had a suggestion. "When you blush, try not to hide it, just continue on with what you're doing. The more you see it's no big deal...the more it will go away on its own."

Chapter Six

Riding the Wave

"**M**y mom and I went out to lunch yesterday and I was going to order for myself...but then I got too nervous," Thomas told Rose. "I could feel my heart racing in my chest."

Rose understood. "That nervous feeling won't last forever. In fact, feelings come and go with our thoughts, like waves in an ocean. That nervous feeling might rise like a wave but then it will go away on its own."

Thomas imagined a wave rising up and crashing on the shore before retreating back to sea.

"So when you feel nervous, like when you're ordering your own food, continue doing it anyway."

"Even if my heart races and my face turns red?"

"Sure. Remind yourself that you're okay...and it won't last.

"Sort of like riding a wave until it goes away," Thomas said.

"Right! The next time you're in the same situation, you might feel a little less nervous. And after a while, those situations that used to make you nervous, might not make you very nervous at all.

"It's just like an athlete who's building strength and endurance by pushing through difficult exercises," Rose explained. "The weightlifter must be able to lift 20 pounds before he can lift 200 pounds, and the runner must be able to run a quarter mile before she can run a mile."

Thomas imagined getting stronger by doing the things that made him nervous rather than avoiding them. "Pushing through my nervousness will be really hard at first," he realized. "Maybe the hardest thing of all."

Rose understood. "It will get easier over time as you discover that you're okay."

It made sense. "So doing stuff even when I'm nervous is another tool for my toolbox," Thomas knew. "It's my *Riding the Wave* tool." Thomas imagined himself riding the wave on a surfboard, all the way to the beach.

Rose nodded. "Riding the Wave will remind you that your nervous feeling is only temporary."

They talked about other ways to feel strong,

like getting a good night's sleep and eating healthy foods, like fruits and vegetables.

"When I go for bike rides, I feel happy," Thomas said. " I can bike more."

"Excellent!"

Rose taught the Tuggles about calm breathing, too. "When we're anxious, our breathing changes, and gets shallow, which can make us feel more anxious. A deep, steady breath that feels like it goes all the way to your stomach is calming."

Rose showed them each how to take slow steady breaths. "Breathe deeply in through your nose, hold

it, and allow the air to expand your stomach. Then slowly breathe out of your mouth.

"When our muscles are tense, it adds to our anxiety too," she explained. Rose taught the Tuggles how to relax themselves by drawing attention to each muscle, then tensing and relaxing it. They started at their feet and worked up their legs, to their hands, arms, and face. They could feel the difference it made in their bodies. Thomas liked the way he felt afterwards.

"You can do these things whenever you want, especially before and during situations that make you feel anxious," Rose said. "You could call them your *Calm Body* tools."

Thomas imagined a big balloon expanding with air, the way his stomach did when he breathed in deeply. He liked the idea of having a calm body, so he would use this tool a lot.

"Are you ready to start using your new tools?" Thomas thought so.

"Where would you like to start?"

"I can volunteer in Miss Clark's class, but only when I know the answer." Thomas knew he would feel nervous...but he decided he would do it anyway.

"I think that's a great place to start. How about this week?"

Thomas was ready.

Chapter Seven

Do Something Different

"I thought of a story." Thomas told his dad as they walked home from the ice cream parlor. The autumn leaves had fallen and winter was knocking at the door, but for the Tuggles, it was never too cold for ice cream.

"Let's hear it."

"Once there was a boy who ate a chocolate ice cream cone every day, just like this one. He went to the ice cream parlor, asked for a chocolate cone, gave them his money and got it. It was easy, especially because he had been doing it for so long."

"That's a lot of chocolate," Mr. Tuggle said.

"Yeah. Eventually, he got tired of chocolate and was ready for a change. There were other flavors to choose from, like vanilla, cookies and cream, and strawberry..."

"What about butter pecan?" That was Mr. Tuggle's favorite flavor.

"Yeah, they had that too. But the boy was

afraid to switch. What if the other flavors weren't any good? So even though he didn't want chocolate anymore, he kept ordering it to be on the safe side. But deep down he really hoped they would give him a strawberry cone by accident."

"Then one day he walked in and guess what happened?" Thomas asked.

"He finally got a strawberry cone by accident?"

"No, he got another chocolate one!" Thomas laughed.

"That's frustrating!" Mr. Tuggle exclaimed.

"I know. But then the next time he went, he noticed that other people seemed pretty happy with their strawberry cones. So, even though he was nervous, he got really brave and asked for a strawberry cone. He took a lick, and loved it."

"He made a change!" Mr. Tuggle said.

"And he finally got what he wanted," Thomas added. "He realized that if he wanted something different, he had to do something different."

"Makes sense."

"It's like with me, dad. I can make a change too."

"What do you mean?" Mr. Tuggle asked.

"Since nobody is *really* looking at me any closer than anyone else, I don't have to worry. I can start doing more stuff."

Mr. Tuggle agreed. "You can be yourself and have fun."

"Yes."

"That makes sense," Mr. Tuggle said. "At first you might feel nervous, but that will go away."

Thomas agreed. "I think I'm ready to join the swim team."

"I bet it will be fun."

"But what if I hate it?" *Ping!*

"Then it's not your thing. But, I would be proud of you for trying something new."

"What if I come in last place?" *Ping!* Thomas was afraid of disappointing his dad.

"I would be surprised if you *didn't* come in last from time to time. Some swimmers will be faster than you and some will be slower."

Thomas was surprised. His dad didn't care about winning at all. He just wanted him to have fun.

"But what if I look weird when I swim?" Thomas asked. *Ping!* That was one of Thomas's worst fears.

"Hmm. Do you *really* think that will be a problem?" his dad asked.

Thomas thought of the magnifying glass and reminded himself that nobody would be looking at him that closely. "Probably not." *Ping!* "Besides, the way I swim *is what it is*."

"Very good!"

Thomas felt proud of himself for using his tools.

"Hey dad, I'm going to volunteer in school this week."

"You can do it."

"I think I can too." *Ping!*

Thomas liked the idea of participating in class.

"I'm so proud of you, Tommy."

Chapter Eight

Here and Now

O n the way to school, Thomas told Bill about volunteering in Miss Clark's class.

"You've got this, Tommy. Everyone thinks you're nice, and you're one of the smartest people in class, especially in math."

Thomas didn't always feel that way because his anxious thoughts got in the way.

"Miss Clark says she'll call on me when I'm ready."

"Cool. Hey, I'm signing up for swim team tomorrow, it'll be fun." Bill figured Thomas wouldn't do it, but he still hoped he would.

"So am I." Thomas was nervous about it, but he also felt a little excited. He had the idea that swim team might be fun after all. *Ping!*

"I'm glad." Bill said. They high-fived.

"Me too."

*   *   *

Miss Clark was reviewing last night's math homework. She asked for three volunteers to go to the board and show their work. Thomas raised his hand. He was practicing his calm breathing, taking slow steady breaths in through his nose. Miss Clark called on him. As he walked to the board, he could feel his heart beating in his chest, and his hands were a little shaky, but he could handle it. The calm breathing was helping. He worked out the math problem, then waited for his turn to explain it.

"I bet I look dumb standing here." *Ping!* His old anxious thought crossed his mind. So Thomas told himself a new thought, one that was more truthful: "Nah, I probably look like everyone else when they wait their turn." *Ping!* He felt better. Then, when it was his turn, he pointed to his work on the board as he talked. Pointing to the board took the focus away from him, which helped.

"I bet my voice sounds funny." *Ping!* Another anxious thought crossed his mind. So Thomas told himself a new thought, one that was more truthful. "I bet nobody cares about my voice." *Ping!* He looked around the room. "It looks like they're just doing their work." He felt better.

After Thomas was all done, Kevin asked him a quick question and the next thing he knew, he was explaining the answer to the question, too. Thomas took his seat. He felt relieved it was over, but also proud of himself. "I did it!" he thought. His hands were still shaking a little and they felt sweaty, but it was okay. And to Thomas's surprise, participating was kind of…sort of…fun.

"Thank you, Thomas." Miss Clark said. She appreciated his help.

Then Thomas realized something—when he was answering Kevin's question, he didn't feel nervous. He wasn't thinking about his voice or whether he looked funny. He wasn't worried about what people were thinking of him at all. All he was thinking about was math. Then he realized something else: "You can only think about one thing at a time!"

It was an amazing, really cool discovery…and another tool for his toolbox. "I'm going to practice thinking about what's going on right now—instead of anything else," Thomas thought. "When the teacher is talking, I'm going to listen to what she's saying… when I'm swimming, I'm going to think about my swim stroke…when I'm working in my group at school, I'm going to pay attention to the topic…and

when I'm playing games, I'm going to think about the goal."

If Thomas was thinking about what was going on right then, he couldn't worry about what might happen later, or what people were thinking of him. It was like a shield that would protect him from anxiety.

Thomas would share his discovery with Rose and his family and call it his *Here and Now* tool. A clock would help him remember to stay in the here and now. And from then on, when he found himself wondering how he looked, he would flip his thoughts back to what was happening *right then*.

Bill looked Thomas's way from across the room and gave him a thumbs up.

Thomas smiled back. He thought he was going to win the game against social anxiety—and he felt hopeful. The more he practiced, the better he was going to get. *Ping! Ping! Ping!*

It made sense.

Note to Readers
by Elizabeth McCallum, PhD

In *The Tallest Bridge in the World*, Thomas experiences extreme fear and anxiety about participating in everyday social situations. These feelings get in the way of his school and extracurricular activities and make Thomas feel self-conscious about almost everything he says and does in front of other people. This pattern of feelings and behaviors can best be described as *social anxiety*. In the book, Thomas works with Rose, a therapist, to build a toolbox of tools and strategies he can use to combat the thoughts that lead to feelings of social anxiety. If you struggle with feelings of social anxiety, there are lots of steps you can take to reduce these anxious feelings, just like Thomas did!

What Is Social Anxiety?

It's normal to feel anxious at times, but when these feelings become so extreme that they stop us from doing the things we enjoy, that can become a real problem. Social anxiety is a term used to describe when a person avoids everyday social activities because he's worried about being judged, or he fears behaving in ways that might bring about embarrassment. Usually people with social anxiety don't have any trouble interacting with family members and close friends, but the idea of meeting new people, speaking in public, or unfamiliar situations can put their anxiety symptoms into high gear. Also, social anxiety is different from run-of-the-mill shyness. People who are shy may feel nervous around new people, but they don't tend to avoid new situations altogether as do people with social anxiety.

Fight-or-Flight

Everyone feels anxious or scared sometimes. In fact, feeling anxious can be helpful in certain situations. Our bodies and brains are hardwired to feel anxious and respond to these feelings as part of our *fight-or-flight* response, which prepares us to act quickly when danger might be near. The fight-or-flight response is a built-in brain response that alerts us of danger by causing certain body reactions so we can protect ourselves. When our brains sense danger, they release adrenaline and other chemicals that cause lots of body changes—things like faster heartbeats and breathing, dilated pupils, sweating, even goosebumps! These are all part of your fight-or flight response, warning you to get ready, because you might be in danger!

A long time ago, the fight-or-flight response came in pretty handy when early humans came across predators like lions or tigers or bears (oh my!). The predator's presence would cause an immediate change in the person's body chemistry, allowing her to either more capably fight off the predator or have the energy to escape.

Today, the fight-or-flight response still keeps us safe from trouble, just different kinds of trouble than our early ancestors used to worry about. Just like our cavepeople ancestors, if our bodies didn't alert us to danger by feeling fear, we wouldn't sur-vive for very long. We'd be walking into oncoming traffic, stepping into open elevator shafts, and eat-ing spoiled food. It's safe to say that the feeling of fear serves a pretty useful purpose in keeping us from doing some pretty dangerous things!

When There Is No Real Danger

When someone has social anxiety, or any type of

anxiety problem for that matter, they will often feel anxious in situations in which there is no real danger at all. Their fight-or-flight response gets activated too frequently, too powerfully, and in situations where it isn't actually necessary. The body's reactions (increased heartbeat, sweating, rapid breathing) can be quite intense; the person experiences the situation as if he was really in danger, and his mind goes through all the associated emotions like fear and anxiety.

Most people with social anxiety have fears regarding their social performance. They tend to feel like they have an "imaginary audience," and that everyone is as concerned with their performance as they are themselves. They also tend to be more self-conscious than average and have an extreme fear of being judged by others. In the book, Thomas was preoccupied with thoughts about what others would think of him, and these worries kept him from participating in some activities that he otherwise really enjoyed. He was worried about his voice sounding funny when he answered questions in class, and he was anxious about looking awkward when he would swim. Thomas had convinced himself that other people were scrutinizing each of his behaviors, although he knew he wasn't judging his peers' behaviors that closely, even when they made mistakes or acted silly.

How Social Anxiety Can Affect Your Life

If you have social anxiety, you probably know that all that worrying about what other people might think of you can be pretty exhausting. It can hold you back from joining in on some pretty cool activities. You might be super focused on all the embarrassing things that could happen if you join a club or a team, and that might make you want to avoid those social events altogether. This can lead to a spiral effect where you choose not to participate in social activities because you're afraid of what might happen, but then you don't get the benefits of participation in those social activities, like building relationships with friends, opportunities for fun, and learning experiences. You might also be left feeling disappointed in yourself for not taking part.

School is an extremely social time for most kids. Kids spend several hours at school each weekday, interacting with peers and teachers. As you may know (or have guessed!), for kids with social anxiety challenges, the social anxiety often rears its ugly head during the school day. Like Thomas in the book, social anxiety can keep kids from participating in school. Kids will often avoid raising their hands to volunteer in class, even when they know the answers to teachers' questions! This can keep you from getting the most benefit out of your academic instruction. It can also limit your access to reinforcement from teachers for answering questions correctly, and potentially mask areas of weakness in which you may need additional teacher help.

How to Manage

Dealing with social anxiety isn't easy, but it can be done, especially with help from others. Therapists (like Rose in the book) can help a person with social anxiety learn to recognize his body's fight-or-flight reactions, and interpret them more accurately for the situation. Therapists can also help people learn a variety of strategies to use when they are feeling anxious. Thomas imagined these strategies as tools he was placing into a toolbox he was building. The tools Thomas gathered may be useful for anyone learning to manage their social anxiety. These tools include, among others:

The *Magnifying Glass* Tool

People with social anxiety often feel like everything they say and do is being judged incredibly carefully by everyone around them. The *Magnifying Glass* tool is the understanding that no one is scrutinizing you any more carefully than anyone else. Once you have this tool, you can relax a little bit and feel more free to be yourself in front of other people.

The *Domino* Tool

This is the understanding that our thoughts affect our feelings, which then affect our behaviors, kind of like dominoes. Thomas thought that his friends would think his voice sounded weird, which made him feel anxious and sweaty, which then caused him to not talk in class. Once he changed his thought to a more accurate one (that people would probably not think his voice sounded weird), the anxious feelings decreased, allowing him to more easily speak up in class. Thought, feeling, behavior…dominoes!

The *Nobody's Perfect* Tool

For kids with social anxiety, the possibility of making a mistake in public can seem like the end of the world. Once you have the *Nobody's Perfect* tool, you can see that even if you were to do something really silly in front of others, life would go on. You will understand that we all make mistakes sometimes, and that's okay! In fact, a lot of times, the only one who notices your mistake is you!

The *It Is What It Is* Tool

Through the story of Ellie, Rose helps Thomas understand that a person's quirkiness can actually be what makes her interesting! Learning to accept oneself for who we are, with all our flaws and imperfections, can be hard. But the closer we come to self-acceptance, the less socially anxious we become. We can stop worrying about what other people might think of us and start thinking about what might be fun! After all, *it is what it is!*

The *Here and Now* Tool

Thomas discovered the *Here and Now* tool on his own! When he helped Kevin with a question in math class, he realized that he didn't get nervous because he was so focused on math. Realizing that you can only think about one thing at a time can help you focus on the here and now—that is, on the activity, instead of on fear of what might happen.

The *Riding the Wave* Tool

One of the most important tools Thomas learns is how to "ride the wave" of his anxiety. Rose teaches him that if he just pushes through despite feeling nervous, the reward is often well worth it. Plus, sometimes when you push yourself to do something that makes you uncomfortable, your anxiety actually goes down while you're focused on the task. And the more you ride the wave through your nervousness, the easier it will become!

Calm Body Tools

Relaxation strategies can help people learn to put their bodies in a calm state to reduce anxiety. For kids with social anxiety, learning and practicing deep breathing, meditation, or mindfulness techniques can be helpful, particularly if practiced before or after stressful social situations.

Once you've filled your toolbox with the tools necessary to combat the harmful thoughts that cause you to feel anxious and fearful in social situations, the next step is to test them out! The best way to do this is to try out new behaviors, ones that may make you feel a little uneasy or nervous at first. In the book, Thomas decided to use his new tools to help him make changes in his life, like joining the swim team and volunteering in math class. He found that using his tools to do these things did lessen his anxiety, but also allowed him to have fun and feel proud of himself for being successful.

Overcoming social anxiety takes hard work, lots of practice, and the courage to face your fears and take part in new experiences. With help, you can fill your toolbox with the tools you need to successfully face your social anxiety, just like Thomas did!

Elizabeth McCallum, PhD, is an Associate Professor in the School Psychology program at Duquesne University, as well as a Pennsylvania certified school psychologist. She is the author of many scholarly journal articles and book chapters on topics including academic and behavioral interventions for children and adolescents.

About the Author

Ellen Flanagan Burns is a school psychologist and the author of *Nobody's Perfect: A Story for Children About Perfectionism* and *Ten Turtles on Tuesday: A Story for Children About Obsessive-Compulsive Disorder.* She devotes her writing to helping children overcome anxiety. She believes that children's books can be a powerful therapeutic tool, and supports cognitive-based interventions for children with anxiety-related issues. Ms. Burns lives in Newark, Delaware, with her family.

About the Illustrator

Anthony Lewis graduated from the Liverpool School of Art with a first class honors degree in illustration. Since then, he has illustrated more than 400 children's books for publishers worldwide, from the simplest baby board books to large 200 page anthologies of myths. During his career, he has drawn many varied subjects, from the life cycle of a frog to the life story of Mozart!

He lives in a small rural village in Cheshire, England with his wife Kathryn, children Isabella, Emilia, and Rory, and two cats, Diesel and Harry.

About Magination Press

Magination Press is an imprint of the American Psychological Association, the largest scientific and professional organization representing psychologists in the United States and the largest association of psychologists worldwide.